# WHAT WOULD WE
# DO WITHOUT JILL?

## M. D. Spenser

Weston, FL

32124-6

This book may not be reproduced in whole or in part, or stored in any type of re-
trieval system, or transmitted in any way or via any means: electronic, mechanical,
photocopying, or recording without permission of the publisher.

Copyright © 2000 by M.D. Spenser. All rights reserved.

Published by Paradise Press, Inc. by arrangement with River Publishing, Inc. All
right, title and interest to the "HUMANOMORPHS" logo and design are owned by
River Publishing, Inc. No portion of the "HUMANOMORPHS" logo and design
may be reproduced in part or whole without prior written permission from River
Publishing, Inc. An application for a registered trademark of the "HUMANO-
MORPHS" logo and design is pending with the Federal Patent and Trademark
office.

ISBN 1-57657-336-2

EXCLUSIVE DISTRIBUTION BY PARADISE PRESS, INC.

Cover Design & Illustrations by Nicholas Forder

Printed in the U.S.A.

To B.K. and D.M.
Friends.

# Chapter One

Jill sat alone in her room, crying.

Everything seemed terrible.

She had decided she was the saddest, dumbest, ugliest girl in town. The only reason she had any friends was because they pitied her.

Why couldn't her life just change? She wanted it to change just as quickly as that — as quickly as she could snap her fingers.

Why couldn't she become someone else? Someone smart and funny and pretty, like her best friend, Molly?

Molly had everything. Sure, Jill was glad for Molly's great luck. But she envied her, too.

Molly had two wonderful parents, both of whom were good-looking and nice. Jill's parents were divorced, and sometimes her mother was nasty to her.

Molly already knew what she wanted to be when she grew up — a newspaper reporter. But Jill had no idea if she had enough talent for any kind of work at all.

Molly had beautiful long, black hair. She had a pretty, slim face, too.

But Jill choked in disgust every time she looked in the mirror. She had awful orange hair and freckles on her face and arms. Her face was *way* too fat.

And she wore horrible black glasses her mother had bought for her.

There was nothing she could do except cry — and wish as hard as she could that she was someone else.

How happy life would be, she thought, if she didn't have to be the same dumb old Jill all the time.

After a while, she blew her nose and dried her tears. Then she sat on the edge of her bed and closed her eyes.

Who would she most like to become, she wondered.

A famous movie star? Think how glamorous

every day would be!

Maybe a famous scientist. Discovering cures for diseases would be so interesting and rewarding, and people would be so grateful to her.

What about a book writer? Imagine how much fun it would be to invent thrilling stories!

But no. Jill decided that, if she could pick anyone in the world to turn into, it would be none of those. She wouldn't choose to be a scientist or a movie star or a writer.

The person she would choose to become would be Molly.

Molly was still a kid, with her whole life ahead of her. And what a life it would be, Jill thought.

It would be filled with cute boyfriends and family celebrations. She'd see exciting events as a newspaper reporter, and maybe meet famous people or travel to foreign countries.

Jill closed her eyes even tighter. So tight they almost hurt.

And she wished. She wished silently over and over, "Let me turn into Molly! Let me turn into Molly! Let me turn into Molly!"

After a minute or two of wishing, she opened her eyes and looked at her arms. And she was amazed!

The freckles were gone!

Not one spot on either arm!

She gasped. Had her wish come true?

She felt her own face — and, yes, it seemed thinner!

She was thrilled! Maybe it *was* true!

Quickly Jill turned towards the mirror over her dresser, looked — and cried out in delight.

It *was* true!

She had wished so hard to become Molly that she had *turned into* Molly!

She would never have to worry about being dumb old Jill again.

Her whole life was about to change forever!

# Chapter Two

But, in the next instant, Jill understood that nothing had changed after all.

She stared at her arms again. They were still covered with freckles.

She realized that her vision had been blurry from closing her eyes so tightly. That's why she hadn't seen the spots for a moment.

Now she felt her face again, but it didn't feel any thinner. Not like Molly's at all.

Her imagination had only made it seem thin and pretty for a second.

And the mirror?

Of course. How stupid could a girl be, she thought.

She had taken her glasses off earlier, when she had started to cry. So when she looked at the mirror, she couldn't see clearly.

She had seen just what she had wanted to see — Molly's face instead of her own.

But she wasn't Molly. Nothing about her life was any different. She was still dumb old Jill!

*Biiing-boong!*

The doorbell rang. Maybe that was Molly, Jill thought. Her friend was coming over so they could walk downtown together.

Jill tried to make sure all the tears were gone from her eyes.

Then she heard her mother yelling.

"Jill, it's Molly! Why do I have to answer the door for your friends?" her mother shouted. "Can't you do anything right? Answer the door yourself next time! You're so stupid sometimes!"

Jill hurried downstairs as quickly and quietly as she could.

"Bye, Mom!" she called sweetly, opening the door. "I'm going out with Molly for a while, OK?"

"Yeah, right! Go out with your stupid friends and do whatever!" her mother said. "I'm stuck here cleaning the dishes while you're out with more of your little buddies!"

"But, Mom — I cooked the dinner tonight," Jill said softly. "You said I didn't have to wash the dishes, too. But I will if you want me to."

"Nah, just get out! I don't care. It's not like I have anything else to do!" her mother said. "*You're* the Miss Popularity, remember? No one ever asks *me* to go out!"

"Uh, well, OK then, I guess. Bye, Mom," Jill said, and quietly closed the door.

The two girls walked down the steps of the apartment building where Jill lived with her mother. Then they headed down the sidewalk into the moonlit night.

Molly looked at her friend and smiled.

"It's OK, Jill," she said. "Your mom doesn't mean all the bad things she says. My mom says it's just because your mom isn't happy, that's all. My mom thinks your mom is kind of jealous. You know, jealous of you."

"Jealous of *me*? That's silly! Why would she be jealous?" Jill asked.

"Jill, come on! Get a clue," Molly said. "*Everybody* is jealous of you! You're the smartest girl

7

in sixth grade. You've got a great sense of humor. And you're by far the best-looking girl in the whole school. All the guys want to be your boyfriend."

"As if!"

"As if, nothing. It's true. Why don't you ever see yourself the way your friends see you?" Molly asked. "Just look at your beautiful red hair! And guys love your freckles. And you're really athletic — strong and coordinated. Can't you see how lucky you are?"

"No," Jill said. "You're the lucky one, not me. You're just too nice to tell me the truth. No one wants to hurt my feelings and that's the only reason they're friends with me. I know that I'm just a boring nerd."

"Girl, if you believe that, you're nuts," Molly laughed. "Your mom is right about one thing — you *are* Miss Popularity!"

"Yeah, right. Anyway, let's stop talking about me, OK? I'd rather talk about something interesting. Like you," Jill said, a wicked smile spreading across her lips. "Or maybe you — and Jimmy Smathers!"

Molly shrieked, and both girls giggled together.

"He really likes you!" Jill teased.

"He does not!" Molly answered with an embarrassed laugh.

"Does too!"

"Does not!"

"And he's *sooo* handsome!" Jill said. Then she imitated Jimmy Smathers walking through school. "Hi, I'm Jimmy and I'm captain of the football team. I'm really cute and I can have any girl I want. But I want *Molly!*"

The two friends exploded in laughter.

"I think Jimmy really likes *you*, Jill! I see him looking at you every time we walk by him," Molly said. "He knows you're the best-looking girl."

"No way, José! It's *you*, girl! Jimmy goes for the brunette type, I think," Jill said. "The other day, I saw him in the hall. He was talking to Marcia Walker, but I can tell he doesn't like her. 'Cause when we walked by, he stopped talking and stared straight at you."

The girls shrieked together again.

"No way," Molly said. "I saw him. He was

looking at *you*!"

"At you!"

"No, at *you*!"

But suddenly, all the kidding and joking stopped. The girls had noticed something as they walked along the quiet street towards the center of town.

Something frightening.

"D-do you see what I see?" Jill whispered.

"Y-yes! I think so," Molly said. "Are they following us?"

"I, uh, I think so. Yeah," Jill said.

A car was casting a large, black shadow on the street beside them. The car stayed close behind them, but it was so quiet that they could barely hear the motor running. The shadow didn't move past them quickly, as a car's shadow normally would. It didn't slow down, either, as if the driver were looking for an address.

The shadow stayed exactly in the same place.

The car was following them — rolling along with its headlights off, just a few feet behind them.

"Walk a little faster," Jill suggested. Then she

grabbed Molly's shoulder. "No, don't look. If we turn around and look at them, they'll know we suspect something. Let's just try to get down the street a little farther and then we'll run into the grocery store."

Before they had a chance to get that far, the car's shadow suddenly sped up. Then a big black Cadillac pulled up right next to the girls.

It was a huge car with windows so dark you couldn't see who was inside.

Molly looked at Jill with fear in her eyes. "They're beside us," she said. "What should we do?"

"Just try to stay calm. They probably don't want to hurt us," Jill said. "And if they try anything, we'll run like crazy!"

With an electric hum, the car's rear window slid open. Jill and Molly looked over but the inside of the car was dark, and they could not see anyone.

The interior of the car seemed as black as a grave.

"Say there, girls!" a man's voice called. It was a rough-sounding voice, the kind killers have in movies. "Hey! Where ya goin' so fast?"

Molly looked at Jill, too afraid to open her

mouth.

But Jill replied in a confident voice. "We're just going up the street to the police station where my father works," she lied. "Can we help you?"

From inside the car, she heard the rough, sarcastic laughter of three or four men.

"Her daddy works at the cop shop!" one man snickered.

"Yeah! The girls are maybe a little scaredy right now, huh? So they're gonna go see daddy, the big tough cop, so he'll protect them!" another man said, guffawing as if someone had just cracked a very funny joke.

The car stopped. Someone stuck a large hairy hand out the window and beckoned the girls to approach by curling one finger.

"Come on over here, girls!" the voice rumbled from inside the car. "Don't be scaredy of us or nothin'. We don't wanna hurt ya."

Another man in the car laughed.

"No, we don't wanna hurt ya or nothing," he said. "We only want to *murder* ya! Ha, ha, ha, ha, ha!"

# Chapter Three

Murder?

Was that what he said? Murder?

Yes, that's exactly what he said!

*Murder*!

The car door opened and out stepped a fat man in dark red clothes.

Molly stood frozen in panic. She couldn't move.

But Jill thought quickly. She grabbed Molly's hand and, pulling her along, started to run.

They only got about two steps away, though, before the fat man snatched both of them by the arms.

"Hey, hey, hey, hey!" he said. "Wait, girls! We ain't gonna hurt ya! We was just kiddin'!"

"Let us go!" Jill yelled. "You have no right to bother us like this! We don't know what you want!"

"OK, OK. Jeez!" the man said, releasing them.

"Sorry, girls. My friends and me got a little carried away with our joke, I guess. We was only gonna ask ya for directions."

"Directions? To where?" Jill asked.

"Well, see, there's this place around here somewheres. We gotta find it," the man said, smiling. "It's called Kalber Concert Hall. They play, like, music there and stuff. You girls know where it is, by any chance?"

"You just want to find the concert hall? Why didn't you just say so?" Molly asked angrily. "You frightened us!"

Jill touched Molly's shoulder to calm her down because she didn't want to upset the fat man and his friends. She just wanted to get away from these strange men as soon as possible.

"Look, mister, it's easy," Jill said politely. "You go down this street for two more blocks and turn right. The concert hall is right there. You can't miss it."

A voice called out from inside the car.

"See, boss? I told ya we was close," the voice said. "I knew these nice pretty little girls could help us. They look the type to go for that music stuff."

"Shut up!" the fat man growled towards the car. "I don't need no help from you guys, ya moron! Keep your big trap shut!"

"But boss, I was only saying . . . " the voice tried to answer.

"I said *shut up!*" the fat man screamed. "Or I'll shut ya up permanent when I get back in that car, understand?" Then he turned back to the girls with a big syrupy smile on his face. "Sorry, girls," he said. "Gotta keep my employees in line, ya know? Sorry we scared ya. Thanks for the help."

Then he walked back to the car with surprising speed, considering how fat he was. The door slammed shut and the car raced off towards Kalber Concert Hall.

"Wow! That was close, huh?" Molly said. "I thought we were goners for sure."

"I don't know if they wanted to hurt us or not," Jill said. "But I didn't want to take any chances so I thought we should be polite. But, hey, Mol — why would weird guys like that want to find our local concert hall? It's closed now. There's nothing going on there tonight."

"You're right," Molly said. "I hadn't thought about that. What do you think we should do? Call the police?"

"Nah, we're just kids," Jill said. "The police won't care if some guys asked us for directions to the concert hall. We'd better go over there ourselves. We'll be real careful. But if these guys are robbing the concert hall or something like that, we should try to find out. Then we'll get the police."

"Yeah, maybe we can call your *dad*, the *police officer*, huh?" Molly said, laughing. "See, that's what I meant about you, Jill. You're so smart to think up a story like that. I was terrified. But you were cool through the whole thing."

"I was just as scared as you," Jill said. "I was only trying to say something that might make them leave us alone. I'm not so smart."

"Oh, yes, you are!"

"Oh, no, I'm not."

"Oh, yes, you are!"

"Oh, no, I'm not," Jill said. "*You're* the smart one, Mol. Anyway, I don't really want to talk about this right now, OK? Let's hurry over to the concert hall and see what those guys are up to."

"Sure, Jill," Molly said, shaking her head. "But some day you're going to have to admit how really cool you are. Hey, wait up! I can't run that fast!"

The two girls trotted two blocks down the street, then turned right towards the concert hall and looked for the black Cadillac. Everything appeared quiet at the auditorium, which loomed dark and empty.

They saw no sign of anyone.

"Maybe they were just going to the house of a friend who lived *near* the concert hall," Molly said. "Besides, it's getting late and those guys gave me the creeps. I want to get out of here. Let's go to the drug store and buy some chocolate, then go home, OK?"

"OK, but let's look around for another minute first," Jill said. "I don't trust those men. I still think they had some reason they wanted to find the concert hall."

"I don't trust them, either," Molly said. "But do we *have* to look around some more? I don't like this, Jill."

"Just stay behind me. Don't be *scaredy*, like that guy said to us," Jill said, smiling.

As they drew near the concert hall, the two girls walked on the lawns rather than the sidewalks, so no one would hear their footsteps.

They looked all around, creeping silently towards the old red brick building where the local symphony orchestra performed great works of music by composers such as Beethoven and Mozart, Bruckner and Bach.

The moon was high. It cast heavy shadows from the tree branches and the telephone poles onto the lawns surrounding the concert hall.

Somewhere in the distance, a dog barked.

"There's nobody here," Molly whispered. "Come on. This is too creepy for me."

"Shhh!" Jill hissed. "If there's anyone here, they must be on the far side of the building. Let's go look."

With Jill leading the way, the girls tiptoed around the building. Then Jill saw something that made her stop dead in her tracks.

18

She stopped so suddenly that Molly bumped into her. Jill turned quickly with her finger to her lips, then pointed towards the concert hall windows.

In a corner of the building that was almost completely hidden by shadows, one window was propped open. The black Cadillac sat parked in the street, its motor running quietly.

Jill felt Molly tug on her arm.

"This is crazy. Let's go call the police," Molly whispered. "They're robbing the concert hall. Maybe they're stealing money — or maybe the musical instruments or something. If they see us, we're dead!"

"Shhhhhhhh!" Jill said. "We'll be all right."

A moment later, two men climbed out of the window. One was the fat man, and behind him came another man.

Jill knew that the hall's windows and doors were always kept locked. Obviously these men had broken into the building.

But one thing struck her as odd. If they really were burglars, she wondered, why did they carry nothing in their hands?

Jill saw no pillowcases stuffed with money

stolen from the concert hall safe. The men carried no bags or boxes full of drums and trumpets and clarinets and other musical equipment.

What were they doing, Jill wondered. Why had they gone to so much trouble to break into the concert hall if they weren't going to steal anything?

The men paused on the windowsill and looked around as if they feared that someone might have spotted them. Their eyes swept the landscape, probing into this corner and that, scanning the area for any sign of movement.

Jill and Molly flattened themselves against a bush, held their breath and tried not to move a muscle. Jill felt her heart beating in her throat.

The fat man's eyes scanned the street where Jill and Molly hid, seeming to search the area house by house and lawn by lawn.

Luckily, the girls were hidden deep in the moon's shadows. The fat man's eyes passed over them.

The men said nothing to each other. They just looked at each other and shrugged, then finished climbing out the window. They hurried back to the black Cadillac and closed its doors softly.

Then the car glided quietly into the night.

# Chapter Four

Police cars sat everywhere, parked at crazy angles. Their flashing lights cut through the night, turning everything around first red and then blue.

Dogs that sniffed for bombs and dogs that sniffed for drugs were snuffling all through Kalber Concert Hall — down every hallway, in every office and practice room, in the auditorium where the musicians performed and around the outside of the building, too.

Police officers swarmed over the building like ants on an anthill, carrying guns and radios and flashlights.

It had been almost two hours since Jill and Molly had spotted the bad guys climbing out the concert hall window.

The girls stood beside one of the patrol cars, still shivering with fear from their encounter with the thieves or whatever the men were. The patrol car's lights throbbed brightly, bathing the girls in pulsing shades of red and blue.

Jill saw a tall, thin policewoman approach.

"You're *sure* you two saw some guys come out of this concert hall?" the policewoman asked. "You're not making this up just to get attention, are you?"

Jill looked at Molly, surprised by the question.

"As if!" Molly said. "We stood right over there and watched a big fat guy and another guy come out that window."

"Like we told you, officer, we followed them here," Jill said. "It didn't make sense that a car full of men were asking about the concert hall when we knew it was closed. We were just trying to make sure they didn't do anything bad to the concert hall, that's all. We're supposed to go there for a big classical concert tomorrow morning with our teacher and some friends from school."

"All right," the officer said. "But if you girls are lying, you're going to be in a lot of trouble. Every cop in town is here right now, looking for evidence.

You'd better hope we find some. You two just stay right here. We may want to talk to you again before you go home."

Jill glanced nervously at her watch. She thought about her mother and her stomach churned. Molly patted her on the shoulder.

"I wish the police would let us call our parents," Molly said. "But don't worry, Jill. Maybe your mom won't be *too* angry that you're out late. The police promised to drive us home as soon as they're done. It probably won't be much longer."

"You're right, Molly," Jill said. "I just hope Mom doesn't get too upset. I hate it when she yells at me just before I go to bed. I'm always tired the next day because I can't sleep much."

Three police officers marched towards Jill and Molly — the same woman as before, accompanied now by two men. They weren't smiling.

"Uh-oh," Jill said. "This doesn't look good."

The first to speak was a man with gray hair and some kind of insignia on his collar.

"I'm Major Roberts," he said sternly.

"You girls are in trouble," the female officer added.

"I'll handle this, Corporal Simmons," the older man said. "Look, girls — we've had more than forty police officers searching this concert hall from top to bottom for two hours. We have found nothing missing."

"We already told you those guys weren't carrying anything when they came out the window," Molly said. "Why are you angry with *us*?"

"We just called to report what we saw, Major," Jill said. "Are you saying we shouldn't have phoned to report a break-in at the concert hall? We saw these guys coming out that window over there — we saw it with our own eyes."

"That's the problem, girls," the major said. "We've dusted for fingerprints and checked for footprints. We've looked at the window for signs of forced entry. But there aren't any. There's no bomb inside the concert hall. No one brought drugs in or out. As far as we can tell, no one even opened that window tonight. I don't know what you two are up to, but I don't like it. Lying to the police is a serious offense."

"*Lying?*" Jill and Molly asked at the same time.

"That's right, girls. *Lying!*" barked Corporal Simmons, the female officer. "I'm afraid you'll both have to come with us to the police station. You are both under arrest for lying to the police!"

# Chapter Five

The rest of the night did not go well for Jill and Molly.

Major Roberts explained that they weren't *really* under arrest. The corporal had gotten a bit too excited.

But they did have to come to the police station and answer more questions. And if they had lied to the police, they might face charges.

It seemed like a nightmare. They were only in the sixth grade and now they were under arrest. Or at least, kind of under arrest.

After they arrived at the police station, the girls were finally allowed to call home. Molly's parents believed her story at once and hurried to the station to help.

But Jill's mother was not nearly so kind. She insisted that Jill must have done something wrong.

"Why would the cops drag you down to the station if you're so innocent?" she yelled into the phone. "You're gonna have to get your*self* out of this mess. I'm in my pajamas and robe. I'm not coming over there until morning, so you can just spend the night in jail. Maybe it'll teach you a lesson. I always knew you'd turn out no good!"

Then she hung up.

Jill cried after that.

"It'll be all right, Jill," Molly said. "My parents will get us out of this. We're not going to stay in this awful police station a minute longer than we have to. Please, don't cry."

The police put Jill and Molly in a small room with one bright light and began to pepper them with questions.

"What were you two *really* doing at the concert hall?" Major Roberts demanded.

"Come on," another officer added. "We know you made up the whole story. Just tell us why you did it and maybe you won't have to go to juvenile detention."

After a while, the police allowed Molly's parents into the small room to join them.

The parents pointed out that both girls were A students. Both were popular with students and teachers. And neither was a liar.

"If they said they saw someone come out that window, then they really saw someone," Molly's father insisted.

Finally, the police agreed to let the girls go home. But they were still under suspicion until they gave a good explanation for their call, Major Roberts said.

Jill blamed herself for everything.

Her stupid attempt to do something good had gone terribly wrong, as usual. It was all her fault, she told Molly's parents.

But they disagreed, and so did Molly.

"Jill was really the brave one, Dad," Molly said. "We would never have seen those bad guys if it hadn't been for her."

"We would have been better off *not* seeing them," Jill said. "I'm so sorry about all this, Mol."

Molly's parents said they were proud of both girls, and took them out for ice cream.

"You were just being good citizens by reporting a crime," Molly's mom said. "It's not your fault the police couldn't find anything wrong."

After that, Molly seemed to brighten up. But Jill still felt unhappy.

That night, she slept in Molly's room. In the top bunk, she tossed and turned for hours.

She just couldn't sleep.

In her mind, she heard her mother's words over and over again: "I always knew you'd turn out no good!"

Lying there in the dark, Jill started to cry.

Mom's right, she thought. I *am* no good. If I were as smart as everyone says, I wouldn't have gotten us into this mess with the police. My mom isn't to blame if her daughter is rotten. I can't stand being me. I hate the way I think and talk and laugh. I hate the way I look. I'm not pretty like my friends say! Molly's the one who's beautiful! Why can't I be more like her? Oh, I wish I could be like Molly! I wish I could just be Molly and never have to be *me* again!"

She cried half the night, then finally fell asleep.

But even as she slept, Jill was restless. She

squirmed and rolled, tossing off her covers.

Just before dawn, she woke up and put on her glasses. She tiptoed out of the room so she wouldn't disturb her friend.

She crept into the bathroom and locked the door. She stared at her own face in the mirror.

How could anyone think *that* was pretty, she wondered.

Her mind roamed over the lives of people she knew, imagining how happy they must be. Her teacher, Ms. Wolfe — she sure looked happy.

Maybe life was better if you were a nice teacher handing out homework to kids. It had to be better than sitting home doing the stupid assignments while your mother yelled at you.

Then there was her principal, Mr. Johnson. He seemed happy, too. He must like walking around with that wooden ruler in his hands, acting tough all day, Jill thought.

Maybe life was better if you were allowed to boss a lot of people around. Maybe that made you feel more important.

But she always came back to the same

thought: Molly was the happiest and luckiest person in the world.

Molly had everything — great parents, great personality, great brains, great looks. How wonderful it must be to live Molly's life!

Suddenly, Jill couldn't stand looking at herself in the mirror for another second. She thought she would scream if she ever had to look at that orange hair again.

So she closed her eyes.

Desperate to feel better, she tried to imagine how it felt to be Molly. She didn't just imagine Molly's face and hair and arms. She imagined Molly's *feelings*.

She imagined feeling pretty and smart, and feeling loved by her parents. She imagined, as hard as she could, what it must be like to feel good about herself.

She stood there feeling all of this more intensely than she had ever felt anything. She stood in front of the mirror for a long time with her eyes closed, feeling Molly's feelings.

She stood there for so long that the sun came

up, sending streams of golden sunshine through the window.

She stood there so long that, without warning, her arms and legs began to tingle. Her face tingled, too, as if her skin were stretching and moving over her bones.

It was a very strange sensation. It felt like her flesh had become sculptor's clay, with someone's fingers shaping and molding it.

What was happening to her?

Jill was frightened — but not frightened enough to open her eyes. She kept them closed until the strange sensation stopped.

When at last it ended, she opened her eyes and stared straight into the mirror.

There in the glass, close up and clear as a bell, she saw *Molly's* face staring back at her!

It was no mistake this time.

No wishful thinking or blurry vision.

In fact, her glasses had vanished into thin air. She had perfect vision without glasses now — just like Molly.

Through some weird magic she couldn't explain, Jill had morphed into her best friend. It was for real.

And now there was no turning back!

# **Chapter Six**

But if Jill was Molly now, where was *Molly*?

The *real* Molly?

Was she still sleeping safely in the bottom bunk? Or had something happened to her, too?

Maybe because Jill had turned into Molly, Molly had turned into Jill. Or maybe Molly didn't exist anymore.

Had she accidentally killed her best friend?

"Oh, no! What have I done?" the new Molly cried. She turned, frantically unlocking the bathroom door. "*Molly!*"

But just as the *new* Molly opened the door to run to her friend's room, the *old* Molly darted down the hall towards the bathroom to see why Jill had shouted her name.

They ran smack into each other — then stood in amazement, nose to nose.

35

For a second, they looked into each other's eyes. Then the truth struck them at the same instant.

"*Aaaaahh!*" they shrieked.

They stopped and looked at each other again, in complete shock. They stared for a moment, as if looking into a mirror. Then they shrieked again.

"*Aaaaahh!*"

"Shhh!" the new Molly urged, pushing the old Molly into the bathroom. "Your mom and dad will wake up. We've got to be quiet!"

The new Molly locked the door as the old Molly shook her head in disbelief.

"Jill? Is that you?" the old Molly asked at last. "What happened to you? Is this some kind of trick?"

"I don't know what happened. And I don't know who I am!" Jill said. "I was just thinking about you, Mol. I was thinking how much I admire you and how great it must be to have your life. And then I opened my eyes and I looked like this. Like *you!*"

They heard footsteps in the hallway.

"Girls?" Molly's father asked. "We heard someone yelling. Are you all right?"

"Yes, Dad," Molly called. "Sorry we woke

you up. I just had a nightmare and Jill is talking to me."

"All right, girls," Molly's father said. "Call us if you need anything. I'm going back to bed."

Molly grabbed Jill by the shoulders and turned her so they faced each other.

They were perfect copies of one another. It was unbelievable!

"This is so weird," Molly said. "You even *sound* like me. But . . . but you're not me, really. *Are* you?"

"I don't know," Jill replied. "But, hey, I've got an idea. You always say I'm better at history than you. What if you ask me a history question you couldn't answer? If I know the answer, I must still have Jill's mind and Jill's feelings and everything. I just *look* like you, that's all. See what I mean?"

"Uh, I *think* so, Jill — uh, Molly, or whatever I should call you," Molly said. "So you want me to ask a history question I can't answer, right?"

"Right. If you don't know the answer and I do, then I'm still Jill."

"Hmmmm, let's see. OK, how about this?

When was World War II fought?" Molly asked.

"That's easy," Jill said. "World War II began in 1939 when Hitler invaded Poland. But the U.S. didn't get into the war until 1941, when the Japanese attacked Pearl Harbor. The war ended in 1945 after the United States dropped two atom bombs on Japanese cities."

"Wow. Well, that answers *that* question," Molly said. "You're *definitely* Jill. So you only look like me. But you're really still you."

"Yeah, right. I'm still Jill inside, but I just look and sound like you," Jill agreed.

"You were a lot prettier the other way," Molly said. "I liked it better when you looked like Jill."

"I think I look prettier this way," Jill said. "But I can't *stay* this way. What about your parents? They don't want a clone of their daughter walking around."

"And what about *your* mom?"

"And what about the kids at school? And Ms. Wolfe? And Mr. Johnson? What will they say?"

"Jill, this isn't going to work," Molly said.

"You've got to go back to being yourself. How did you turn into me, anyway? Maybe you should try the same thing. But, like, in reverse or something. Please, Jill! Before Mom and Dad find out."

"I'll try," Jill said. "I'll see if I can remember everything I did. I'll do the same stuff and maybe that'll turn me back into myself."

So she closed her eyes and imagined looking like herself again. She concentrated very, very hard. She tried to will herself back into being Jill, even though she really liked looking like Molly.

She knew that Molly was right. Everyone would be confused and angry if she looked like Molly forever.

She tried to think and concentrate and will herself back into her own body. She willed so hard that she even held her breath, trying to force more energy into her mind.

She held her breath so long that she began to turn purple.

But nothing happened. There was no change at all.

She tried again. And then again, still willing

hard and holding her breath.

Nothing.

She looked at Molly hopelessly.

The real Molly and the fake Molly faced each other and stared again.

"It's no use," Jill said. "I tried with all my willpower, Mol. I think I'm stuck! I wanted to be you so bad that now I'm going to look like you forever."

Her lip began to quiver and soon both girls broke down into frightened sobs.

# Chapter Seven

They cried rivers of tears.

They held each other and hugged like sisters, sobbing until they could sob no longer. Then they sniffled and hugged again.

Finally they dried their tears and blew their noses. Crying wasn't going to help explain this mess to Molly's father and mother.

Or to Jill's mother.

Or to anyone else.

They had to calm down and figure out what to do. They thought long and hard. Both girls offered suggestions.

Maybe Jill should just move into Molly's room and they could tell everyone they were twins. Or maybe Jill could just explain that she'd had plastic surgery.

But none of the ideas made any sense. There

was no chance that any of them would work.

At last, though, Jill remembered something. Her eyes lit up and she snapped her fingers.

"You know what?" she said. "I forgot that when I turned into you, I was trying to feel your feelings. I imagined feeling exactly what you must feel inside you. That was when I morphed into you. It wasn't willpower that did it. It was *feeling your emotions*."

"Wow, that's really weird," Molly said. "But you go, girl! Try to feel what *Jill* would feel inside. Maybe then you'll change back into yourself."

Jill closed her eyes again. But this time she didn't hold her breath or will herself into Jill's body or anything like that.

She just tried to remember feeling like no one else but Jill. She felt orange-haired and freckled and ugly. She felt unpopular and guilty and responsible for everything that went wrong.

She felt these feelings intensely.

Her arms and legs began to tingle. Her face tingled too, as if her skin were stretching again. It was the same strange sensation as before.

When the sensation finally stopped, Jill opened her eyes and found Molly staring at her.

Molly looked just as stunned as when she had first seen Jill that morning walking down the hall in Molly's body.

"It worked, Jill," Molly whispered. "Wow! You just morphed back into yourself — right before my eyes! *Wow!*"

Jill turned to the mirror. It was true.

She had really morphed back into herself. She had the same hair she'd always had, the same freckles, the same everything.

"How is this possible, Mol?" she asked. "People just can't turn into other people, and then turn back into themselves again. Can they?"

"*You* can! I knew you had, like, this great brain, Jill. But this is really heavy duty," Molly said.

For a few minutes, the friends said little to each other except one word: "Wow!"

Then they were interrupted by loud knocking on the front door. Who, Jill wondered, would come pounding on the door before seven in the morning?

The girls hurried downstairs to answer the

door.

When they opened it, they found Jill's mother standing there. She looked furious. Her hair was rolled in curlers and her mouth was turned down into a fierce frown.

"You snotty little brat!" she snapped, glaring at Jill. "I got up early to go to the police station to bail you out of jail. And they tell me you spent the night with your little friend here. I told you I wanted you in that jail overnight and that's what I meant! I wanted to teach you a lesson!"

"I'm sorry, Mom," Jill said. "I didn't mean to upset you."

"*Upset* me?" her mother said. "You made me so mad I should beat the living tar out of you, you brat!"

At this moment, Jill understood that there were some things that even brain power could never change. Yes, somehow she could change her appearance and her voice.

But she could not change her mother. She was stuck with the same mother forever.

Jill's mother reached back as if she were going

to slap her daughter across the face. Molly's jaw dropped open, unable to believe what she was seeing.

"Mom, please!" Jill begged. "Wait 'til we get home. I'm sorry, Molly. I didn't want you to see this."

"You brat!" her mother shouted, raising her hand again.

"No! Don't hit her! Jill didn't do anything," Molly said, putting her body in front of Jill for protection.

"Get out of my way or I'll slap you too!" Jill's mother yelled. Then she grabbed her daughter by the arm. "I'm taking you home now! And when we get there, I'm going to slap you clear into next week! I'll put some sense into that stupid, ugly head of yours! You're in big trouble now, you no-good brat!"

# Chapter Eight

The angry mother yanked her daughter's arm hard.

Jill hung her head and cried as she started to follow along, walking behind her mom.

But Molly yelled: "Stop it! Leave her here!" She grabbed Jill's mother's arm, but the woman pulled herself free.

"You stay out of this, you stuck-up brat!" the woman bellowed.

At that moment, Molly's father came running down the stairs.

"What on earth is going on here?" he demanded. "What do you mean, screaming insults at these girls in my home! I want you to get away from this house — *now*!"

"This is none of your business!" Jill's mother spat back. "It's between me and my kid! Nobody else has any right to interfere."

"You have no right to abuse anyone in our home, not even your daughter. Now leave this house or I'll call the police," Molly's father ordered. "And Jill is staying right here. You should be ashamed. Now *go!*"

Jill's mother looked at her daughter with hatred.

"I'll deal with you later," she hissed, then slithered off into the morning sunshine.

Molly's parents dried the girls' tears and helped them calm down.

"Don't worry, Jill, darling," Molly's mother said gently. "You can stay with us as long as you need to. We won't let your mother treat you that way again."

"I love my mom," Jill said sadly. "But I can't talk to her when she gets like that. I should have listened to her and stayed at the jail, I guess. She's a single parent raising me all alone. I know that's hard. It's really my fault that she yelled at me like that."

"Don't be ridiculous," Molly's mother said. "It's *never* a child's fault when an adult yells hurtful things. That's verbal abuse. And it can be just as painful as physical abuse. Don't blame yourself. You did the right thing by coming with us last night. Now you two had better hurry along and get into the bathroom. I know you both have to be at the concert hall in an hour. Today's the day you're going to the symphony!"

Luckily, Jill and Molly were about the same size, so getting ready for the concert was no problem. Jill just borrowed a few clothes, including some dressy pants and a pretty sky-blue top.

Then they ate a delicious breakfast of bacon and eggs that Molly's mother had cooked. Jill thought the whole kitchen smelled warm and loving.

Finally the girls walked towards Kalber Concert Hall, where all their problems had started the night before.

Jill felt terrible about everything.

She felt she was to blame for forcing Molly to follow the bad guys to the concert hall. She felt she was to blame for getting them both in trouble with the police. She felt she was to blame for morphing into Molly's body, frightening her best friend half to death.

She felt she was to blame for leaving the police station after her mother had told her to stay overnight. And she definitely felt she was to blame for all of her mother's awful screaming at Molly's home.

The two girls didn't talk much. Jill was too sad to talk and Molly didn't seem to know what to say.

Jill walked slowly, with her head down. She stepped off a curb to cross the street without looking.

With no warning, a huge black car raced around the corner.

"*Jill*!" Molly hollered. "*Look out!*"

But it was too late.

The car now was only a few feet from Jill. Some crazy driver was speeding through a red light.

And he was about to run Jill over!

# Chapter Nine

The car was only a second away from hitting Jill.

At that instant, Jill twisted her head to see why Molly was screaming. As she twisted around, her foot slipped on a spot of oil that had spilled on the pavement.

She fell on her back, hard, dropping to the ground as if someone had pushed her.

The fall saved her life. The car missed her by less than an inch, then sped away without stopping.

"You crazy jerk! You almost killed her!" Molly shouted at the car. Then she helped Jill to her feet. "Are you OK, Jill? I thought you were going to get hit for sure."

"I'm OK, I think," Jill said, brushing off her clothes. "I hope I didn't rip your top, Mol. Wow, that was so close! I didn't even see him."

"Don't worry about my top, Jill. It's not ripped. Are you sure you're OK?" Molly asked. "But, hey . . . wait a minute. I think that was the same car those bad guys were driving last night."

"Really? A black Cadillac?"

"It sure looked like the same car to me," Molly said. "Do you think those guys came back to try to run us over on purpose? Maybe they know we called the police."

"I don't know, Molly," Jill said. "But I don't want to wait around to see if they come back and try again. Let's get to the concert hall fast, OK?"

They ran the rest of the way and trotted up the steps towards the large metal door.

That's when they saw it.

The black Cadillac was parked on a side street beside the concert hall. It was definitely the same car the bad guys had driven the night before.

And it was probably the same car that had just almost run over Jill.

The girls looked at each other for a moment, unsure what to do.

Then Jill grabbed Molly's hand.

"Come on, Molly!" she said, pulling her friend inside the concert hall. "We've got to tell someone that those crooks are out there. This is way too weird. Those guys are up to something bad, that's for sure."

"I'm right behind you, Jill!" Molly said. "Maybe *now* the police will believe us."

They raced down the hallway towards the building's front office, sprinting as fast as they could, with Jill running ahead and Molly following close on her heels.

But as she rounded the last corner before the office, Jill skidded to a stop. She hurried back to hide behind the wall.

"Shhh!" she whispered. "It's those same guys. I saw them."

"Here? Inside the concert hall?" Molly asked worriedly.

"Yeah, it's the fat guy, and there are three other guys with him," Jill said, peeking around the corner. "The same ones as last night. They're going into the front office right now. And they don't look happy. Whatever they want in that office, I don't think anyone who works here is going to like it."

"I have a feeling no one inside this whole concert hall is going to like it," Molly said. "Especially us!"

# Chapter Ten

Soon the girls heard people yelling inside the office.

It was so loud they could hear every word, even with the door closed.

"Listen, bud! We want them *now*, got it?" one of the bad guys shouted. "We got no time to wait around for you to change your mind!"

"I *told* you already! I don't have them! I found them this morning in one of the practice rooms our musicians use, and I turned them over to the police," a man replied angrily. "Get out of this concert hall, you fools! The police are coming back to talk with me. I hope they catch you — but not inside this hall. We have a symphony concert to give very soon, a special performance for some middle school honor students and a large group of senior citizens. Now please leave!"

"*Sure* the cops are coming, pal," another crook said. "We heard that one before. Like last night from some cute little girls who got all scaredy and says their big tough daddy is a cop. Right, boss? Ha, ha, ha!"

"Shut up, moron!" said the voice of the fat man. "Now look here, pal. We're gonna get what we left here last night, see? And if we don't get it, we'll take *you* with us instead. *Got me?*"

The voices grew softer. Jill couldn't hear anything except mumbling.

Suddenly an announcement blared over the concert hall's public address system.

"If I can have everyone's attention please! This is Maestro Colin Andrews speaking, the conductor for today's special morning concert," the man said over the loudspeakers. "I'm afraid we have a situation that will delay our music-making. Some men are pointing a gun at my head right now. They're gangsters. And they're ordering me to tell you that everyone must stay in their seats. They will shoot anyone they find roaming the halls or wandering anywhere near the pay phones. Musicians must stay out of the way, backstage. Please listen to me, everyone! It's a matter of life and death!"

Jill and Molly looked at each other. Things were even worse than they had imagined!

Still, they decided they had to do something to help rescue the conductor, Maestro Andrews.

But what?

# Chapter Eleven

They wanted to call the police. But they didn't carry cell phones, like some of the girls did.

Besides, Maestro Andrews was right. If the police raced over here and surprised the bad guys inside the concert hall, audience members might get shot by mistake.

They decided the best plan was to scare off the bad guys somehow.

Jill suggested setting off the fire alarms. That would ring bells all over the concert hall, and maybe frighten the crooks away.

Then Molly remembered Jill's new mental powers. She suggested that, since Jill already had morphed into her, maybe Jill could morph into other people, too.

They were thinking this over when they suddenly realized that they could put their two ideas together to come up with an even better plan.

"We'll set off the fire alarms, like you suggested," Molly said. "But before we do, you can morph into Maestro Andrews. That means there will be two of him. When the bad guys hear the alarm and come out of the office with the conductor, they'll look down the hallway and see *another* conductor who looks just like him!"

"You're a genius, Mol! If that doesn't scare them away, nothing will! They'll think they're going nuts," Jill said.

"Yeah, or maybe seeing double. Anyway, it's got to terrify them. I know it would terrify me."

"I just hope I can morph into Maestro Andrews," Jill said. "I've only done this thing twice. I'm not sure if I can do it again or not."

"You've got to try, Jill," Molly said. "Remember how you did it before. You have to imagine how the other person *feels* — the person you want to morph into. You can do it, girl. I believe in you!"

Jill closed her eyes. She tried to feel what the symphony conductor might feel inside him. She started to feel responsible for all the music performed at the concert hall. She felt responsible for training the musicians to play together well and for dealing with out-of-tune oboes and off-tempo trombones.

And she began to feel pride, too — pride in a job well done, in giving a performance that makes an audience stand up and cheer.

She felt these feelings intensely. Her arms and legs and face began to tingle. This time, the skin all over her body seemed to stretch as if it were made of rubber.

Soon, the sensation stopped and she opened her eyes.

Molly was staring at her.

"It worked, Jill!" Molly said. "Uh, I mean Maestro Andrews. Uh, I mean, Jill."

"Wow! And just listen to me, Mol!" Jill said. "My voice is all deep and everything, just like Maestro Andrews sounds. It really feels funny."

The girls tried to smile, but they knew there was no time to lose. This was serious business.

The two of them hurried down the hall to the fire alarm. Jill reached up with Maestro Andrews' strong hands and pulled it down as hard as she could.

Instantly, the alarm sounded, echoing down the hallways and nearly deafening them.

Jill and Molly ran back to the hallway outside the front office.

"You hide behind the corner, Molly," Jill said in her new deep voice. "I'll just stand out here in the open. They'll see me right away when they come out. That'll be a sight they won't forget. *Two* Maestro Andrews instead of one!"

The office door sprang open and all four gangsters darted into the hall.

A crook wearing a goofy green baseball cap was holding the conductor by the collar of his tuxedo and pointing a gun at his back.

The fat boss and the three others looked around furiously, trying to see who had set off the alarm.

That was when they spotted Jill — the fake Maestro Andrews.

"Boss, *look*! There he is again!" said the crook in the baseball hat, with his mouth open wide. "The conductor guy! Only I got him right here in my hands. But he's over there, too!"

He almost dropped his gun out of fear. The plan was working! The crooks were about to run away.

At least that's what Jill thought for a moment.

Until the fat boss glanced at the real Maestro Andrews, then at the fake Maestro Andrews, then back at the real Maestro Andrews. And, unfortunately for the girls, what he saw didn't scare him.

It made him angry. *Very* angry.

His eyes looked sinister and heartless.

"Hey, what kinda game ya tryin' to play on me?" he snarled at the real conductor. "Ya think I'm stupid or what? Just 'cause ya got a twin brother, that don't mean nothin' to me. We ain't leavin' this concert hall 'til we get what we left behind last night!"

Then he reached under his jacket and pulled out a gun.

And he pointed it directly at the fake Maestro Andrews's chest — right at Jill's heart!

# Chapter Twelve

Just then, the sound of sirens echoed through the air.

Sirens went off everywhere —down the street, up the street, to the north, to the south, and even, it seemed, up in the air.

*Wauuw-waauuw! Wauuw-waauuw!*

It sounded as if fire trucks, ambulances and police cars were all hurrying at once towards Kalber Concert Hall with their sirens blaring.

*Wauuw-waauuw! Wauuw-waauuw!*

Jill had felt sure that, after she pulled the alarm, every firefighter and ambulance driver and police officer in town would race to the concert hall. Everyone would know that if there was a real fire, children and senior citizens could be in danger.

The sirens were so loud that it sounded as if every emergency vehicle in the county was arriving.

Fortunately, they were also loud enough to distract the crooks.

The fat boss forgot his anger over the second Maestro Andrews. Instead, he ran to the window with his gun pointed, ready to shoot. The other crooks ran with him, dragging Maestro Andrews with them.

"Jeez, boss," the crook in the green hat said. "Look at all them cops and fire trucks and stuff. We ain't never gonna get outta here now."

"Yeah, we're in a big pickle now, boss," said a tall crook with a long dark beard.

"We gotta start blastin' our way out now, boss!" said a third crook, who had a mean face and a body as muscular as a bodybuilder's. "Before *all* the cops get here. We just got mostly firemen out there now. They'll all get scaredy as soon as we start shootin'."

"*Shut up, ya morons! All of ya!*" the boss shouted. "I'm thinking about it, OK? Just keep your traps shut!"

As all this happened, Jill and Molly ran down a long hallway towards the women's bathroom. Jill thought they would probably be safe in there until they could decide what to do next.

And she already had another plan.

"Look, the police are outside, right?" she said. "What if the crooks think the police are *inside* the concert hall too? I'll morph into a policeman and maybe that will frighten the bad guys. Maybe they'll surrender to me because I'll be standing there with a badge and gun."

"Yeah — or maybe they'll kill you!" Molly argued. "It's too dangerous, Jill! Let the real police catch these guys. We should just find a place to hide where we'll be safe."

"But the crooks have Maestro Andrews as a hostage. They might shoot him or kidnap him," Jill said. "As long as I have this power to morph, I've got to use it to frighten these guys. Everybody in the concert hall is in danger, Molly. We might be able to do something that will save lives — maybe even the lives of our friends from school!"

Finally, after more talking, Molly agreed. But she said the plan scared her to death.

Both girls understood that they couldn't spend more time talking about it, though. It was time for action.

Quickly, Jill tried to imagine the feelings of the tough police officer she had met the night before, Major Roberts.

She felt confident and experienced and self-assured. She felt a need to protect people, and keep them safe. She felt a hint of fear, at not knowing who lurked around the next corner or how dangerous the next assignment would be. And she felt concern over what would happen to her family — to Major Roberts's family, that is — if he were hurt or killed in the line of duty. She felt all this and more.

She was getting better at morphing. She could do it faster and with less effort now.

Immediately, she felt the tingling and the stretching. In a few moments she had become Major Roberts!

At least, she *looked* exactly like him — big and strong and tough.

"OK, Molly, wish me luck!" she said in the major's commanding voice. "I'll need it. Now remember, you're going to your seat in the audience and you're going to stay there, right? You'll be safer.

And I'll know where you are if I need you."

"I still think I should go with you, Jill," Molly said. "Let me stay close in case you need help. Besides, if I watch what happens, I can write a story for the newspaper about it. It'll be my first report as a real newswoman."

"No way, Mol," Jill said. "I look like a policeman, and I've got a gun. You don't. Besides I saw a TV show that said crooks don't like to shoot cops. They're scared of what will happen if they get caught."

"I just hope this gang of crooks saw the same TV show," Molly worried.

As Jill — the fake Major Roberts — walked slowly down the hall, she could hear the real police outside the building. By now, the authorities had discovered that there was no fire.

Police helicopters hovered overhead. SWAT teams scampered across the concert hall lawn, ducking behind cars and bushes. They carried rifles and wore black clothes and bulletproof vests.

Crowds of newspaper, TV and radio reporters took notes and talked into microphones. Traffic was blocked in all directions.

"Come out with your hands up!" a police officer shouted through a bullhorn. "We don't want to hurt you. And we don't want anyone else hurt either! If you come out now, we can ask the judge to go easier on all of you!"

"You ain't gettin' us outta here!" the fat boss screamed. "Not unless we see all ya cops gone and we get a car! Understand me? We won't hurt anyone unless we have to! But we got this concert hall full of little kids and old people! We'll use 'em to get away if we have to!"

Jill was shocked. The crooks really were willing to hurt people to escape, she thought. They might hurt her friends — and maybe even Molly.

That was all she needed to know.

Without thinking about it, she ran down the hallway towards the front door. It felt odd to run inside someone else's body — with long legs, big feet, and no clunky glasses bouncing around on her nose.

She had 20/20 vision, just like Major Roberts.

She rounded a corner and saw the gang looking out a window at the police. The boss was giving orders to his men. The crook in the green hat still had his gun pointed at Maestro Andrews.

Jill drew the gun from her holster and aimed it at the gang.

"Put your hands up! You're under arrest!" she barked. "I want you to put down your guns and let Maestro Andrews, uh, let the conductor there go! *Now!*"

She felt like a character in a police movie.

But she was still Jill inside. She didn't know anything about being a policeman. And she could never really shoot a gun at anyone. Not even at a gang of bad guys.

The instant the gangsters saw her, though, every one of them pointed his gun at her.

The crooks didn't hesitate this time. After all, this was not just a clone of Maestro Andrews standing in the hallway. This was a police officer running at them with his gun drawn.

At the same moment, all four gangsters fired their guns at Jill.

Suddenly she faced a terrible choice.

She would either have to kill someone — or *be* killed!

# Chapter Thirteen

For a split second, Jill thought about shooting at the crooks.

But she couldn't do it. She knew instantly that she simply couldn't kill anyone.

So she did the only thing she could do. She ducked for cover.

Luckily, she was in Major Roberts's tall, strong body. When she pushed off with those long legs, she found herself flying through the air like Michael Jordan.

Bullets whizzed around her, skipping off the floor and breaking chunks of cement from the walls. But somehow, every bullet missed her.

Every bullet, that is, except one.

As she soared through the air towards the doorway of the conductor's office, a single bullet grazed her lightly on the arm.

She was hit!

She came crashing down inside the room, then jumped up, slammed the door and locked it.

She checked her arm. There was only a tiny spot of blood. Her wound was no deeper than if a cat had scratched her. This was nothing serious.

But something else *was* serious: The gangsters were banging on the door!

"Ya lousy cop!" the boss gangster yelled. "Come outta there or we'll blast our way in!"

"You're dead meat, cop!" the crook in the green hat shouted.

Jill knew he was right. She *was* dead meat — unless she could think up a new plan fast.

Like, very fast!

Because now the gang began to shoot at the lock. In a moment, the door would swing open!

And when the gangsters burst in, they would find Jill sitting on the floor looking like a police officer.

A police officer in big trouble.

A police officer who might soon be very, very dead!

## Chapter Fourteen

*Bwaaammm!*    *Bwaaammm!*    *Bwaaammm!*
*Bwaaammm!*

Four gun shots.

The lock on the office door dropped off. The door swung open. And, very slowly, four gangsters peeked around the corner.

They were looking to see how badly the police officer had been shot. And to find out if the officer was going to try shoot them back.

So imagine their shock when they found no police officer at all. Instead, they found a woman.

No one else — just a gray-haired woman.

"What the . . . Hey, what gives here, boss? Who is this?" the tall crook with the beard wondered.

"All right! Where's the cop?" the boss demanded. "Stop wastin' our time, sister, and tell us where he's at. We know he's in here."

The woman smiled sweetly.

"As you can see, gentlemen, there's no police officer in here," she said.

At the sound of that voice, Maestro Andrews looked around the corner too. The crook in the green hat still was pointing his gun at the conductor.

"Who are you?" Maestro Andrews asked. "And . . . but . . . what are you d-doing in *my office*? I was in here right before all this began and turned the lights out myself. How did you get in here?"

"I'm a teacher at the middle school. I teach many of the honor students here today. I just came in to try to meet you, right before you made your announcement about staying in our seats. So I stayed in here and then the shooting started," the woman answered. "It nearly frightened me out of my wits!"

Of course, this really wasn't a teacher. It was Jill.

She had quickly morphed into her own teacher, Ms. Wolfe, when the gang began shooting at the door.

The moment she had changed bodies, the bullet wound had healed.

It was gone. No more bleeding.

And right after morphing into Ms. Wolfe, Jill had removed the cover from a heating vent in the conductor's office.

This was part of her latest plan to outsmart the bad guys. Maybe she could make the fat boss believe the policeman had escaped through that vent.

The boss glared at the fake teacher.

"Listen, sister, I want answers and I want 'em now," he snarled. "We know a cop ducked in here, because we shot him. Here's the blood right on the floor. Now tell us where he went or we'll give it to ya, understand me?"

He pointed his gun at Jill.

"I should think you could see for yourselves," Jill replied calmly. "If you bother to look, you'll see that heating vent cover on the floor over there. I'm very much afraid your police officer escaped through there, gentlemen. He's gone."

"Wow, boss. He was pretty smart for a cop, wasn't he?" said the muscular, mean-faced crook. "They don't think so quick most times. Usually cops only wanna shoot us. And eat doughnuts."

74

"All right then, sister. Out in the hall," the boss ordered, motioning towards the door with his gun. He looked at Maestro Andrews. "You too, pal. Get out there with your new teacher buddy."

The symphony conductor and Jill walked into the hallway near the front door of the concert hall. Every gang member had a gun pointed at one or the other of them.

"What are we gonna do, boss?" the crook in the green hat asked. "Blast 'em? I ain't been able to kill nobody in at least a month. Let me do it, OK, boss? Please?"

"No, we ain't gonna kill 'em!" the boss snapped. "We're gonna find those diamonds we left in this building last night. I don't believe this guy turned them diamonds over to the cops. He's got 'em — or maybe he give 'em to somebody else. And we're gonna find out who!"

*Diamonds*, Jill thought. The crooks came into the concert hall last night to hide some diamonds.

So *that's* why the gang came out of the concert hall window empty-handed, she thought. They weren't taking something *from* the concert hall. They were leaving something *in* the concert hall instead.

But why? Why hide diamonds in a concert hall, of all places?

Then she remembered hearing some friends talk the previous afternoon about a big jewelry store robbery.

Of course, Jill thought. That was it!

The expensive jewelry store in town had been robbed yesterday afternoon — and this must be the gang that pulled off the heist.

They were probably worried about getting caught. So they had found someplace to hide the diamonds overnight. Someplace they thought was safe. And what better place than a concert hall? A concert hall is a place where gentle, honest musicians work hard to play great music that the public loves to hear. No one would think of looking there for stolen diamonds.

But the conductor must have found the diamonds in the morning and turned them over to the police, just as he had told the bad guys.

"I'm afraid I can't help you." Jill told the crooks. "I certainly don't have your diamonds."

"No, she doesn't," Maestro Andrews said. "As I have explained many times now, I have given them to the authorities. You can do whatever you want to me, but I can't produce something I don't have. Don't you imagine I'd be glad to turn them over to you if I had them? The only thing I want is for all of you to leave this concert hall as quickly as possible."

"He's got a point, boss," the black-bearded crook said. "Even if he got them diamonds hid somewheres, he couldn't keep 'em anyway. The cops would ask too many questions now. So why wouldn't he just give 'em to us and let us take off?"

The fat boss just stood silently for a moment, staring into Maestro Andrews' eyes.

"Yeah, ya know — I think he is telling us straight, boys," the boss finally said. "And that's too bad for the music man and Miss Teacher-lady here. 'Cause now they're no good to us. Unless they can help us get outta here alive with all these cops around."

"What do you plan to do with us?" Maestro Andrews asked. "Why can't you let us go now? Your diamonds aren't here any longer. Just leave this concert hall and make your getaway, or whatever you people call it these days."

"We're taking you two as hostages, understand me?" the boss replied. "You both are coming out that front door with us, see? You're gonna be our cover, standin' right in front of us. Then you're both comin' along on our getaway. Unless the cops try to shoot us. And then they'll just shoot you instead!"

"Whatever happens, I know one thing for sure," the crook in the green hat said with a nasty grin as he looked toward the conductor and Jill. "I sure wouldn't want to be in your shoes right now! Ha, ha, ha, ha!"

## Chapter Fifteen

"I'm sorry, gentlemen. I'm afraid I won't be able to go with you," Jill said in a voice that sounded just like her calm, confident teacher.

"Hey boss! The teacher says she can't make it right now. But she says thanks anyway! Ha, ha, ha!" laughed the green-hat crook.

"Yeah, maybe she's got something better to do," the muscular gangster sneered. "Or maybe she's just a little scaredy now, that's all."

"Huh? What do ya mean ya ain't comin'?" the boss snapped. "You're comin' where we tell ya to come, understand me?"

"I'll be happy to do whatever you ask," Jill replied. "Except that I'm afraid I have a case of the flu right now. And I'm suddenly feeling — well, rather sick."

"Sick?" the boss asked.

"Yes," Jill answered, holding her breath between words so that her face would turn red. "I'm terribly sorry, but . . . well, I'm afraid I'm going to . . . well, *vomit* if I can't get to a bathroom quickly!"

By now, her face had turned as red as an apple.

"Oh, jeez, lady!" the boss said. Then he looked at the muscular gangster. "Hey, take her to the bathroom to get sick. Then bring her back here, got it? And make sure there ain't no one in there with her first, understand?"

The crook grabbed Jill's arm and together they hurried down the hall to the women's bathroom.

"Hey! Any ya ladies in there or what?" the gangster shouted into the bathroom. "Hold on, sister! Don't lose it on me yet. I just gotta make sure there ain't nobody in there. Then ya can go toss your cookies into the toilet or wherever."

The crook looked around the bathroom and found no one inside. Then he told the pretend Ms. Wolfe to go in.

"Hurry up and get it over with," he ordered. "We can't wait around here all day just 'cause ya get all sicky on us now. Make it snappy, lady."

Jill rushed into a stall and locked the door. She pretended to throw up, making a bunch of gross sounds.

But she wasn't really sick. She had dreamed up another plan to help defend the crowded concert hall from the gangsters.

Outside, helicopters were still hovering. SWAT teams were in place, with their rifles ready to fire if the crooks appeared outside. Reporters still crowded behind police barricades.

"This building is completely surrounded!" a policeman shouted into his bullhorn. "There is no possible escape! Come out with your hands up!"

As she heard all this commotion, Jill began to think about Molly. Yes, Molly would be the best person now, she decided.

She was going to become Molly again, just as she had early that morning.

Jill knew for sure now that she could morph quickly whenever she wanted.

So, very soon, she was *feeling* like Molly. She tried to feel exactly what Molly might be feeling —

the security of having a loving family and a good home. And of course, the fear over being trapped inside a concert hall with a gang of desperate criminals.

Right then the tingling and stretching started. In just a few seconds, Jill had become her best friend once more.

She looked in the mirror and laughed to herself.

This should work, she thought. This dumb gangster won't know what to think.

Then the fake Molly simply walked out of the bathroom and waved at the crook as if this was just a normal day and the crook was just another music lover waiting to hear the concert.

Of course, she didn't get far before the gangster stopped her.

"Hey! Where'd *you* come from, missy?" he demanded. "There weren't nobody in that bathroom a minute ago!"

"Well, sir, I guess you didn't see me. But I saw you," Jill replied sweetly. "I'm sorry, but I had to use the bathroom. Now if you don't mind, I'll just go back to my seat and join my schoolmates until all of this violence is over. Is that all right with you?"

The gangster was so shaken and confused that his face turned gray. He stared blankly into space, as if someone had hit him in the head with a board.

Then he motioned with his gun that the girl was free to go.

Jill glanced over her shoulder long enough to see that the crook was going back into the bathroom to look for the teacher.

Wait until he finds that Ms. Wolfe isn't in there, she thought. He'll probably be so *scaredy* he'll think the concert hall is haunted.

She hurried down the hallway, eager to begin the best part of her latest plan against the gang. She went into a dark practice room, a place with a piano and drums and music stands, and closed the door. Then she began to morph again.

This time, though, she wasn't morphing into the conductor or her teacher. She wasn't morphing into her best friend or even into a police officer.

She had a better idea — an idea she felt sure would confuse the crooks more than anything else she could do.

She was about to morph into a gang member!

Instead of fighting these crooks from outside their gang, she would fight them from the inside.

She had decided to morph into the mean-faced, muscular crook who had taken her to the bathroom.

She thought it was a great idea, but she also understood that it was dangerous, too. If the fat boss found out she was the fake gangster, not the real one, she wouldn't be inside the gang anymore.

She would be inside a coffin, buried six feet under the ground.

# Chapter Sixteen

It was contrary to her nature, but Jill concentrated on feeling mean. She felt nasty and greedy and filled with hate. She felt as if the world had done her wrong, and she wanted to hurt it back.

No sooner had the tingling and stretching begun than she was finished. She looked just like the mean-faced, muscular gangster.

It was time to test her plan.

She hoped to cause total confusion within the gang. When the boss saw *two* gangsters who looked exactly alike, he wouldn't know which was which and who was who.

Whom could he trust? Which was the pretender? And how had somebody turned into an exact copy of the strongest crook in his gang?

Surely this time Jill's morphing tricks would shake up everyone in the gang — including the boss.

Maybe the crooks would get so upset they would make a mistake. Then the police could arrest them. Or maybe the gang would become so afraid they would just turn themselves in.

It was worth trying.

She strode down a long hall towards the front door, where the gangsters still waited with guns drawn. She sort of rolled from side to side as she walked, looking tough, and she could feel the muscles in her arms.

As she looked down the hallway, Jill could see some of the bad guys gathered far at the other end of the building.

But before she got anywhere near the door, someone rounded a corner and yelled at her. It was the tall crook with the long black beard.

"Hey! Where the heck ya been anyways?" he yelled at Jill, who of course looked just like his fellow gang member. "The boss is really ticked off! He sent me to find ya. He wants to get outta here with that guy when we're done. What took ya so long with that teacher? And hey, where *is* that teacher-lady anyways?"

"The teacher? Oh, yeah, right. She's still real sicky in the bathroom, the dumb lady!" Jill answered quickly, sounding just like the muscular gangster. "I gotta go back for her in a second. But wait a minute. What do ya mean, 'when we're done?' Done with what?"

"With beating up the kids, ya dope," the bearded crook said. "You was around when the boss told us his plan. Remember? I know you're stupid, but jeez! He told us to beat up a whole bunch of kids and even a few old folks before the getaway. Ya know, whap them with our pistols and bloody them up, some kids and old ladies sitting around the audience. Then everybody will be so busy helping fix up all them hurt people, we'll be able to scram outta this dump without gettin' caught. And we'll take the conductor guy with us for extra insurance."

Jill was stunned. The gang planned to injure many students and senior citizens. Hit them on the heads with pistols. Bruise them. Hurt them badly.

It was unbelievable. Incredible!

These crooks were going to harm some of her friends! Possibly even Molly!

And unless Jill could stop them somehow, they were going to do it very soon!

# Chapter Seventeen

The situation was getting more desperate every minute.

Jill could imagine all the cuts and bruises, all the fear and screaming, all the tears and bandages. Kalber Concert Hall would be the scene of one of the cruelest crimes she could imagine, the terrorizing and injuring of innocent children and senior citizens.

But she couldn't let her fear show now. She tried to act as tough and cruel as the muscular gangster would.

"Oh, yeah," she growled. "I remember the plan. When do we start anyways? I ain't hurt no one in a long time. Except — hey, wait! We gotta talk to the boss again first."

"What for? We got our orders. Let's go start bashin' these brats!"

"No, we can't do it yet, see? 'Cause he ain't

told us if we got to bash the musicians sittin' back-stage, too!" Jill said. "I ain't knockin' out nobody unless the boss says so."

"Hey, yeah! Yeah, you're right! I ain't thought about that!" the bearded crook said. "He ain't said nothin' about no musicians. Maybe he meant to bash them too!"

"I dunno about you, pal. But I ain't gonna make the boss mad at me for messing up his orders," Jill said. "Come on. Let's check it out first."

They walked together towards the rest of the gang.

But now Jill had to think up a new plan fast. She couldn't depend on simple confusion to keep the gang from clubbing members of the audience. She just didn't know exactly what the new plan was yet.

Now they were only a few yards away from the gang.

The boss was looking out the front window at the police. The crook in the green hat still pointed his gun at Maestro Andrews.

And the mean-faced, muscular crook was there, too, making sure his gun was full of bullets.

"Hey!" Jill hollered, pointing at the muscular gangster. "What gives here? Who the heck is this chump? Hey, are ya bringin' in a new guy, boss? Where'd ya find some mug that looked just like me?"

The boss and two of his men stared at Jill, then at the real crook.

Their mouths fell open. They looked back and forth, again and again. At Jill, then at the real gang member, then at Jill again. The boss rubbed his eyes, as if he were seeing things.

But the mean-faced, muscular crook seemed more shocked than anyone. When he saw Jill, his face went blank for a second.

Then he looked horrified, as if he'd seen a ghost.

"Hey, b-boss! What's up with this building?" he muttered. "First this teacher disappears in the bathroom. And now there's some guy who looks just like me. I . . . I don't like this, boss!"

"Yeah, this place gives me the creeps, boss! Let's get outta here!" the green-hat crook said. "Strange things are happenin'! Like *real* strange, ya know?"

Jill knew this was her chance. She had to make them believe she was the real gangster.

"Boss, hey! How come you're doin' this to me? Who is this guy?" she demanded, pulling a gun from under her jacket. "And how come he's got a gun just like mine?"

"I dunno who this mug with me is," the boss mumbled. "Uh, I mean I don't know who you are. I mean I don't know which one of ya is doin' what. But somethin's wrong here somewheres. And when I find out, somebody ain't gonna like what I do to him!"

"I think we should blast 'em both, boss," the crook in the green hat suggested. "Ya know, just to be safe."

"Thanks, buddy!" the muscular gangster said.

"Yeah, thanks, pal!" agreed Jill, the fake gangster.

"Nah, I gotta better idea! Come here, the two of ya!" the boss ordered the identical crooks. "I ain't got time for no games. One of ya is wearing a mask or something — and I'm gonna take it off right now!"

He pinched and pulled and tugged on the real

crook's face. But of course nothing came off.

Then the boss slowly turned to Jill.

"OK buddy, so if it ain't him," he snarled, "the fake one has gotta be *you!*"

He grabbed Jill's cheek and started to yank it. Then he clawed at her chin. Then he yanked at the skin around her eyes and forehead.

Jill knew she had to act tough, just like the real crook. No crying or complaining. So she just stood there and let the boss pull her face in all directions.

But nothing came off her face, either.

"Hey, what is this anyway? Is this some new cop trick or what?" the boss snapped. "I know that one of you two is a fake. One of you is tryin' to spy on my operation. *And I don't like that, understand me?*"

He was furious now. The fat boss looked like he wanted to kill whichever crook was the faker.

But he looked confused, too, as if he had no idea how to find out who the faker was.

At last, one of his men spoke up.

"Hey, boss, I got a idea," the bearded crook

said. "Why not ask 'em what was the first bank we robbed together? If one of 'em can't tell ya, then he's the faker for sure."

The boss paused, glaring at Jill and the muscular crook.

"Ya know, for once ya gotta good idea," he said. "Yeah, that's what we'll do. We'll ask 'em to name the first bank we robbed. They can take turns and whisper the answer in my ear."

"Make 'em tell ya real soft so they can't cheat, boss," the bearded gangster said, looking at his gun fondly. "Then if ya want, I'll take care of the faker for ya. Yeah, I'll blast that big faker two or three times right in the head!"

# Chapter Eighteen

The boss pointed at Jill first.

He was about to demand the name of the first bank his gang robbed — and Jill didn't know! Once they realized she was the fake gangster, they would shoot her.

She tried not to tremble with fear.

She couldn't bluff her way out of this mess. She couldn't even morph her way out of it, either.

Or — or could she?

Maybe she could.

Maybe morphing was her *only* hope of avoiding two or three bullets in the head from these bad guys.

The boss stared suspiciously at Jill. He demanded the name of the bank, then leaned near her lips for the answer.

As he did this, Jill began her quick-change

routine. She started to feel the feelings of other people — to feel them so strongly that quickly she morphed into them.

She morphed into one shape then another as the boss stood only two inches from her.

First she morphed into Maestro Andrews.

Then she morphed into Ms. Wolfe.

Then she morphed into Major Roberts.

Then she morphed into Molly.

Then she morphed into the mean-faced, muscular gangster again.

Finally, she morphed back into herself. She was Jill once more.

She did all this in the space of thirty seconds.

Just imagine the reaction of the gang — and poor Maestro Andrews, who also watched these wild changes!

Those five witnesses weren't merely shocked. They looked stunned, amazed, and disbelieving. No words can describe the shock and horror that showed on their faces.

The fat boss's eyes almost bugged out of his head.

"*Yaaawwhh!*" he shrieked, jumping back from Jill.

The other gang members all bellowed in terror, too.

And Maestro Andrews passed out. He just fainted and dropped to the floor like a rock.

The boss and his gang were too terrified to run. They were too terrified to shoot. They just stood, staring and hollering and pointing their fingers.

As they did, Jill turned and sprinted down the hallway. Soon she had escaped from the sight of the gangsters.

But she knew this was not the end of the terrible danger at Kalber Concert Hall. Far from it. Soon the gangsters would begin beating students and senior citizens to create mass confusion.

Then they would make their getaway, holding Maestro Andrews as a hostage, while the authorities were distracted by the need to help the injured audience members.

As she ran, Jill wondered what she possibly could do to help stop these heartless crooks.

Her power to morph had worked wonderfully

so far.

It had confused and frightened the gangsters, and delayed them from kidnapping Maestro Andrews and harming her classmates.

But now, she thought, it would not work again. There was no way. If she tried any more morphing tricks, the boss would simply shoot her.

Jill knew that the only person who could save her friends and the rest of the audience now was — Jill.

Just plain old dumb Jill?

Yes, it was true.

Just Jill!

She was the only person who knew the gang's plans to harm the audience. And she was the only person with any chance to help prevent this bloody deed.

Quickly, she darted into an empty practice room and sat down to think.

What could she do?

She was just one kid against a gang of violent thieves. One young girl inside a large concert hall.

And that's when she came up with another

plan.

Jill suddenly realized that she had to get *everybody* in the audience to fight this gang. Kalber Concert Hall, after all, had more than two thousand people who had come to hear classical music that morning.

If all of them stood up to these four crooks at the same time, maybe the bad guys would finally have to leave.

It might work, Jill thought, tapping a finger against her cheek. It just might work.

But it was risky.

If her plan failed, she and half the audience in the concert hall might end up lying in their own blood.

# Chapter Nineteen

The best people to talk to first about this new plan, Jill decided, were her own classmates.

For one thing, they all knew her very well. For another, her best friend was there.

Molly would be in the audience waiting for her, ready to help in any way. What a great friend, Jill thought as she ran down the hallway. Molly was the best!

Something else went through Jill's mind as she ran.

Maybe Molly and the other kids in school were at least a little bit right about her. Maybe she wasn't quite as dumb as she had always believed.

Jill had to admit that she was fighting off this awful gang with nothing but her brains — and, of course, her amazing new power to morph into other people.

Maybe she was a bit smarter than she had thought.

She hoped so.

Because now even her morphing powers were useless. She knew she had only her own wits to rely on in this desperate effort to save the audience of Kalber Concert Hall.

When she finally reached the main entrance to the ground floor seating, she rushed inside and closed the door behind her. All her classmates were huddled together in several rows of seats near the front of the empty stage. Their teacher, Ms. Wolfe, who had come to the concert with her students, was comforting them.

"Jill!" Molly shouted. "You're OK! I heard gunshots and I was really worried they had hurt you!"

"Molly wanted badly to try to help you, Jill," Ms. Wolfe said. "But I insisted she stay here with the other students where she was safe. But I'm so relieved you're not injured. Molly told us all about your efforts to fool these thugs."

"Yeah, and I told everybody about this incredible power to morph you have," Molly said. "It

101

took a lot of explaining, but they all believe me now."

"Yes, I've read about such abilities," Ms. Wolfe said. "I understand that some people in certain African cultures can change into the shape of other people. But it's incredible that one of my students can actually do this. Just astonishing!"

For a minute, some of the students forgot their danger and called to Jill, asking her to morph into someone else.

"Come on, Jill! *Please!*" Jeannie Abbott pleaded. "You're always so smart! I just *know* you can do this. Just like Molly told us!"

"Wow, can you really turn into someone else whenever you want? You're amazing, Jill!" Bob Knotts pointed out. "Can you show us how you do it?"

Ms. Wolfe held up her hands to quiet every-one down. But it was Jill who took charge of the situation.

"Listen, you guys," she said. "I can show you this morphing stuff later on, if you want. But we're in really big danger. And I have an idea that might help us get out of it. It's risky, but I think it might work.

We have to hurry, though. There's not a second to waste!"

She explained everything she knew about the gangsters. She told everyone about the plans to injure a bunch of students and seniors and then kidnap Maestro Andrews for the getaway.

Finally, she told them about *her* plan.

"We have to all march together down the hallway and face the gang — every one of us in the whole concert hall!" she said. "I'm pretty sure if we get two-thousand people to stand together and order these creeps to leave, they'll go. I've seen how they think. We can frighten them off if we do something they don't expect."

"But what if they just shoot us all right there in the hall?" Ray Noble asked. "They might just mow us all down. Maestro Andrews warned us to stay in our seats."

"I don't think these crooks will do that," Jill said. "Maybe they're killers when they *have* to kill. But they're not mass murderers. I don't think they'll want to kill hundreds of kids and senior citizens. I know it's dangerous for us to try this. But I really think they'll get scared and run off."

"We don't really have much choice either," Molly added. "Unless someone can think of something better, this is our only chance. If we do nothing, lots of our friends will get their heads bashed, for sure. And if the police storm the concert hall, bullets will be flying everywhere, and someone might even get killed. If we try Jill's idea, we just could all make it out of here in one piece."

Ms. Wolfe said Jill's plan worried her, but finally even she agreed to try it. "It's probably the only way we can stop these thugs from battering a bunch of children and older folks," she said.

Jill told her classmates that they should all walk quietly to the back hallway behind the stage at two o'clock sharp.

Then she rushed around the audience to talk to other groups of people, explaining her plan to the rest of the students and to the senior citizens. Somehow she got them to listen to her — and to trust her, too.

Even though she was a stranger to most of them, Jill persuaded everyone to show up with her classmates at two o'clock. They all realized it was their best hope.

"I heard what the other kids were saying about you before you walked in," said Bill Ryan, an eighth grader from another school. "You sound like you really have it together. I don't think we have any choice except to follow your idea — unless we want to stay here and get beaten up!"

"You seem like such an intelligent, pretty girl," added Cathy Lute, a senior citizen sitting nearby. "And I can see how popular you are with your school chums. I just believe that you wouldn't lead us into any unnecessary danger. Since you've been around these crooks and I haven't, I believe you know best, dear."

Soon Jill stood in the back hallway, watching the clock. The minute hand inched toward the top of the dial to mark a new hour.

Very quickly it was exactly two o'clock.

Jill saw both stage doors quietly begin to open. Without a word, kids and senior citizens started filing into the back hallway.

They had all tiptoed out of their seats and

across the stage towards the meeting point. They came from everywhere inside the large auditorium — from the left, from the right and from the center aisles, from the front row and from the balcony.

Streams of students and senior citizens filled the stage, making almost no noise at all. Jill heard just a slight shuffling of feet and one or two stifled coughs as they edged into the back hallway.

No other sounds.

She was amazed how silent two thousand people could be when their safety depended on it.

And she knew their safety — and hers — really did depend on silence.

They also depended on the strength of her plan. All she could do now was pray with all her might that the plan was good.

With herself in the lead, she motioned that it was time to go. Very slowly, the whole huge mass of people began to move as one down the hallway towards the front door.

Soon a concert hall full of unarmed students and senior citizens would face four armed gangsters who were desperate to escape from the police.

The moment of truth was at hand.

# Chapter Twenty

The gang still waited at the front door.

Jill could see them now. They were watching the police, talking angrily about the SWAT teams and helicopters.

They were also talking fearfully about "that little girlie who changed into everybody else, right when we was about to blast her!"

Jill knew the gangsters were waiting for just the right moment to begin their getaway plan. Then they would stride into the audience and start clubbing people.

And they would run away from the police with Maestro Andrews as a hostage.

But now the crooks were going to face something that wasn't in their plan, Jill thought. They were about to meet a lot of determined people who wanted them gone.

Jill turned to face the students and seniors with one finger at her lips, reminding everyone of the need for silence.

Two thousand people crept forward step by step, almost on tiptoe. Outside, the police blared surrender demands over their bullhorns. Helicopters whirred overhead.

Inside the concert hall, the gangsters heard no sound at all from the large group moving down the hallway.

The audience inched onward. Soon they stood no more than ten feet behind the crooks.

Then they packed themselves closely together, shoulder to shoulder, as Jill had instructed. They formed a wall of people, an unbroken barricade against four deadly invaders.

"Excuse me," Jill said to the gangsters. "I'm sorry to bother you. But we're afraid you'll have to leave now."

"Jeez, boss!" the crook in the green hat shouted. "It's that kid what changed into all them other people! I don't like this building, boss. It's too weird for me!"

"Yeah, let's get outta here, boss," the mean-faced, muscular crook cried. "Maybe this girlie is gonna change us into frogs or something! She's one spooky kid! I'm scaredy to stay around here!"

"*Shut up, you morons!*" the fat boss growled. "I saw what this kid done, too. But I don't care. I don't believe my own eyes, understand me? She's just some punk who knows some stupid magic tricks."

"But boss, even you was scared when you saw her changing into . . . " the tall crook with the black beard began.

"I said shut *up!*" the boss interrupted. "I ain't scared of nothin'. And I sure ain't scared of no bunch of snotty brats and old dried-up has-beens. Not even a *smart* snotty brat like you, girlie."

"I think you *are* afraid of me," Jill said calmly, though she felt more terrified than ever before in her life. "And I *know* you're afraid of all of us. You have more than two thousand people here, old people and children. Are you going to shoot everyone?"

"Maybe we will, kid!" the boss snarled. "Startin' with you, Miss Troublemaker, ya rotten brat! You're dead, *understand me?*"

"Don't push these men, child! They're very dangerous!" Maestro Andrews pleaded. "This is very brave, but they'll shoot you! They'll shoot you and all the others in cold blood!"

Jill could feel her courage melting like an ice cube on a summer sidewalk.

But she took a deep breath and tried to stop her legs from shaking. Then she spoke again.

"They won't shoot us, Maestro Andrews," she said. "Because if they start, they'll have a mob of two thousand people on top of them in a second. They might kill me and a few others. But they can't shoot us all before we jump on them like a swarm of wasps."

"Yeah, and you'll also have two thousand witnesses to your murders!" Molly shouted. "You'll all go to prison for the rest of your lives! Then you'll be sorry you ever came to Kalber Concert Hall!"

Now other students began to yell at the gangsters — and then senior citizens began yelling too.

"Yeah, get out of here!" one of the students snarled.

"Leave us alone! Or we'll arrest you ourselves

and hand you to the police!" a gray-haired man shouted.

The three gang members looked at their boss with fear in their eyes.

"Hey, boss, maybe we should make a break for it," the crook with the black beard suggested. "I think I'd rather take my chances with the cops!"

"This don't look too good," the green-hat crook agreed. "This building is way too weird!"

Even the boss was starting to waver.

"Look, uh, folks," he stammered. "Get back in your seats or there's gonna be real trouble. I'm, uh, tellin' ya now. Get outta here — go!"

But his eyes no longer looked heartless and sinister. They looked afraid.

"No, *we're* telling *you*," Jill answered, pointing her finger at the boss. "Get out of our concert hall and leave us alone. We came here to listen to music. You have no right to be here and no right to threaten us. You're not going to hurt anyone."

The boss tried to aim his gun at Jill. But he couldn't seem to do it. His hand trembled like a leaf in the wind. His gun dropped to the floor with a thud.

Slowly, Jill stepped towards the gang. The wall of students and seniors stepped right behind her.

The gangsters glanced around like cornered animals. Suddenly the mean-faced, muscular gangster began to run.

He threw down his gun and bolted right into the arms of police officers gathered outside the front door. They slapped him in handcuffs and led him to a patrol car.

Jill and the other students walked slowly closer to the remaining gangsters.

"We all want you to go," Jill said. "*Now! Understand me?*"

The boss and his two remaining men looked at each other hopelessly.

Then they turned and put up their hands. All three walked outside and gave themselves up to the police.

They had been forced into surrendering, just as Jill had hoped.

In less than a minute, all four gangsters were in handcuffs and on their way to jail. As the last gangster disappeared into a police car, Maestro Andrews started to cheer.

"It's over!" he bellowed, pumping his fists in the air. "Yessss! We're free!"

Then he patted Jill on the back and kissed her forehead. "We owe it all to you, young lady. I don't even know what you did. And I sure don't know *how* you did it. But it worked!"

A huge cheer rang out from the students and seniors. They crowded around Jill to give her the thanks due a hero. They slapped her back and shook her hand, and some of them hugged her and kissed her on the cheek.

The biggest hug of all came from Molly.

"You did it, girl," Molly said, beaming. "All just by using your great brain. I'm so proud of you. Now I hope you'll finally stop talking about how dumb you are. You're not only the smartest, prettiest, most popular girl in school. You're the bravest, too."

Jill felt her face get red. Compliments always embarrassed her. But this time she didn't respond by putting herself down, as she always had in the past.

Instead, she said, "Thanks, Mol," and left it at that.

As other friends thanked her, she even thought to herself: Maybe I'm not such a rotten kid after all. Maybe I really am a little better than I thought.

When the police finally entered the concert hall, Maestro Andrews told them about all that Jill had done, and about the courage she had inspired in the other students and adults.

Jill stood around for a long time answering questions from police officers and reporters about how she helped end the siege of Kalber Concert Hall. She even introduced Molly to a reporter from the local newspaper.

"Molly wants to be a reporter like you," Jill said. "She's smart, and she writes really well. Maybe she can help you write the story about what happened at the concert hall today. She saw everything that went on here."

"That's a great idea," the reporter said. "Maybe Molly can write a first-person story, explaining what it felt like to be inside the concert hall with a gang of killers. Would you want to do that, Molly?"

"I'd love to!" Molly replied. "And I'll also

write about my best friend who saved a lot of people from being hurt today. Jill is the hero of this story."

Soon, frightened relatives and friends of the audience members began to arrive. They rushed in and grabbed their loved ones, hugging them and kissing them and asking if they were hurt. Many of the relatives cried — and when the children and seniors finally understood they were safe, many of them cried, too.

Molly's mother and father were among the first to arrive. They wept when they saw her. Then both parents hugged her at the same time.

They squeezed her so hard that Jill wondered whether Molly could breathe. But Molly looked just as happy to see her parents as they were to see her.

And Molly cried just as hard as they did.

Nearly every student's parents showed up. All except Jill's mother. She was nowhere in sight.

As the reporters hurried off to write their stories, the hero of the day stood alone in the hallway.

Jill felt lonelier than she had ever felt before. She felt like an orphan, with no one who loved her enough to find out whether she was dead or alive.

The feelings overwhelmed her, and she started to cry.

Nothing has changed, Jill thought. Nothing is any better now than it ever was.

I am still the same old dumb Jill, somebody no one really loves.

# Chapter Twenty-One

Molly noticed Jill's tears right away. She and her parents had lingered after the others had left.

She rushed to her best friend and hugged her again.

"It's OK, Jill," she said. "It's all over. Everyone's safe now. The gangsters are gone."

Molly's parents tried to comfort Jill, too.

"It's all right, dear," Molly's mother whispered. "You've been through a terrible thing today. You go ahead and cry."

Jill dried her tears and shook her head.

"I'm not really crying because of what happened today," she said softly. "I'm crying because my mom isn't here. She doesn't love me. I was always afraid she didn't love me. Now I know for sure."

"No, that's not true, Jill," Molly replied with a smile. "There's a reason your mother isn't here. Mom and Dad just told me everything that happened. But you were talking to the reporters and I couldn't tell you until now."

"What do you mean, Mol?" Jill asked.

"Your mom loves you, Jill," Molly said, "But she needs some help, bigtime. Now she's going someplace to get it."

"That's right, Jill," Molly's mother said. "Your mother is a very unhappy woman, dear. We knew we had to do something after she threatened to hit you this morning. So Molly's father and I went over to your apartment and talked with her. She cried and told us how deeply she loves you. But she is an angry person, and she takes her anger out on you. She can't help it."

"We told your mother about a friend of ours who counsels women like her," Molly's father said. "She went to see him this morning, before anyone knew about the danger at the concert hall. Your mother checked into a hospital this morning, Jill. It's a place where they can make her better."

"So my mom's really sick?" Jill asked.

"Yes. But she'll get over it, dear," Molly's

119

mother said. "In the meantime, we want you to live with us. You can sleep in Molly's room. You're a wonderful young lady, Jill. But you could never believe it because your mother always said such terrible things to you. She didn't mean them, though."

Molly's mother opened her pocketbook.

"I have a letter for you from your mother" she said. "She wrote it before she checked into the hospital."

Jill took the envelope and opened it. The letter was in her mother's handwriting.

This is what it said:

*My darling Jill,*

*I'm so sorry to leave you this way — so suddenly. But I understand now that I was making your life awful. Please forgive me. I love you more than I can tell you.*

*I know that I have big problems to work out in my life. I need help to do this. But when I'm done, I'm going to bring you back home to me and never say another nasty word to you. Never. And I will never threaten to hit you again.*

*You are the best daughter on earth. I know*

*that — and I want you to know I really feel that way. Forget all the angry words I said to you over so many years. Believe only these words now, the words in this letter. They will tell you how I truly feel.*

*Pray for me, Jill. And know that I will think about you, and I will miss you every day until I come home.*

*With so much love,*
*Mom*

Jill wiped a few tears on the back of her sleeve. But this time she was smiling.

"Wow," she said. "This is a beautiful letter. And all of you are such wonderful friends."

"I think it's going to be great having you live with us for a while," Molly said. "We'll be just like sisters now. Just think how much fun we'll have together in the same house all the time!"

"It really will be nice, Molly," Jill said. "I feel like we are sisters anyway. Except there's one thing I hope you won't ever ask me to do again."

"What?" Molly asked.

"I don't want to morph into anyone else ever again," Jill said. "I know everyone wants to see me do it. But I just can't. Is that OK?"

"No prob, Jill. Besides, this morphing stuff can make things pretty complicated when you think about it. And pretty weird," Molly said.

"For sure, Molly. Morphing was an awesome thing to do for a while," Jill admitted. "But I think I'll be a lot happier from now on just being Jill."

The two girls looked at each other and smiled. Molly put her arm around Jill's shoulder.

"You're the best, Mol!" Jill said.

"No, *you're* the best, Jill!" Molly said.

They laughed for a moment.

"I think we're both wrong," Jill said. "I think we*'re* the best — best *friends*, that is!"

"Best friends, for sure," Molly agreed. "Best friends for life."

# LOOK FOR OTHER

HUMANO MORPHS

# DEEP TROUBLE AT DOLPHIN BAY

It looks like another bummer of a summer for Derrick Granger. His father, a marine researcher, is taking him on a field trip to a dolphin study site in the Florida Keys. Ten-year-old Derrick, a bookish boy who's fascinated by Greek mythology, doesn't even know how to swim.

But soon after they arrive at the center, Derrick overhears a conversation in which terrorists are plotting to kidnap the dolphins and use them to deliver nuclear explosives around the world unless they are paid billions of dollars. No one believes Derrick, and he feels powerless to stop the terrorists—until he stumbles across a strange seashell that gives him the power to transform into the Greek god Poseidon, ruler of the seas. Derrick has a fighting chance against the terrorists now—as long as he can steer clear of the family feuds on Mount Olympus.

# LOOK FOR OTHER

# THE SECRET OF BEARHEAD HOLLER

Growing up in Bearhead Holler, deep in Kentucky's Appalachian Mountains, Amy Fay Jones had always been poor. There was a sketchy myth in her family about a long-lost fortune, but the only person who insisted the story was true was Amy's senile grandmother.

When the grandmother, overcome with poverty and despair, stopped talking and eating, Amy decided she had to find out the truth about her history. She spun sixty years back in time and morphed into her grandmother as a 12-year-old girl. She learned about the coal—and the diamonds—discovered deep beneath the family's craggy land. And she ran into the evil speculators trying to bilk her great-grandparents out of the mine.

Can Amy use her 90's knowledge to outwit the villains and change her family's fate?